FRED & ANTHONY'S

HORRIBLE, HIDEOUS
BACK-TO-SCHOOL
THRILLER

By ESILE AREVAMIRP
With ELISE PRIMAVERA

Hyperion Paperbacks for Children/New York
An Imprint of Disney Book Group

THIS BOOK IS DEDICATED
TO THE HOLLAND KIDS—
JOHN, NORA, AND
ANDREW—AND NOT YOU!

TAP
TAP TAP

First Edition
1 3 5 7 9 10 8 6 4 2

Printed in the United States of America
ISBN 978-0-7868-3684-0
Library of Congress Cataloging-in-Publication Data on file.
Visit www.hyperionbooksforchildren.com

RAINDROPS KEEP FALLING ON MY HEAD Words by Hal David; Music by Burt Bacharach © 1969
(Renewed 1997) NEW HIDDEN VALLEY MUSIC, CASA DAVID and WB MUSIC CORP. All rights
reserved. Used by permission of ALFRED PUBLISHING CO., INC.

RAINDROPS KEEP FALLING ON MY HEAD From BUTCH CASSIDY AND THE SUNDANCE KID
Lyrics by Hal David; Music by Burt Bacharach © 1969 (Renewed) Casa David, New Hidden
Valley Music, and WB Music Corp. International
Copyright Secured. All rights reserved.

FOURTH BOOK!

4

I DON'T KNOW HOW
MANY MORE OF
THESE I CAN TAKE.

ME, EITHER.

CONTENTS

FRED AND ANTHONY MIRACULOUSLY ESCAPED.

THEY ALSO MET A GHOST WHO LIKES TO WRITE.

THAT'S HOW WE GOT THE TITLE FOR OUR FIRST BOOK:

FRED & ANTHONY ESCAPE FROM THE NETHERWORLD

GET IT?

I OFFERED TO WRITE THESE STUPID CHAPTER BOOKS.

BUT THE THING IS, FRED AND ANTHONY KEEP ENDING UP IN THE NETHERWORLD.

LIKE WHEN WE WENT TO FIND *HIM*.

OCSDD GHOST

I'M *REALLY* A ZOMBIE.

CANDY & FLOWERS CONDOS

HE LIVED HERE.

BUT

CANDY & FLOWERS CONDOS

MANIAC TOWERS

OCSDD = OBSESSIVE COMPULSIVE SUPER DEGERM-O DISORDER

THAT WAS OUR SECOND BOOK!

THE DEMENTED SUPER DEGERM-O ZOMBIE

IT WAS MORE WEARING THAN WINSOME.

THEN
WE WENT TO CAMP PLENTY WAMPUM. WE DID A LOT OF CANOEING. . . .
LAKE GITCHIÉ LAGOONIÉ
BUT THE LAKE WAS *REALLY* THE BLACK LAGOON.
GLUG! GLUG!
TO NETHERWORLD
BACK IN THE NETHERWORLD, FRED AND ANTHONY MET THE HEINIE GOBLINS.
HIYA.
AND THAT'S WHY THEY CALLED THEIR THIRD BOOK:
FRED + ANTHONY MEET THE HEINIE GOBLINS from the BLACK LAGOON
GET IT?
THE QUESTION IS: HOW MUCH MORE OF THIS CAN FRED & ANTHONY TAKE?
IF THIS BOOK KILLS YOU—CAN I HAVE YOUR BASEMENT?
SO ANNOYING!
HE'S SO ANNOYING.

SWEET BASEMENT

Summer was over, and the boys were finally home from the horrible, hideous camp they had been sent to.

HELLO, FOOD-STAINED LA-Z-BOYS.

HELLO, DINGY CINDER-BLOCK WALLS.

IT'S ACTUALLY MORE BEAUTIFUL HERE THAN I REMEMBER.

I WAS JUST THINKING THAT.

Now that Fred and Anthony were home, they could finally catch up on all the movies, Pez, and Chex Mix they had missed.

It was time to go back to school.

Fred and Anthony went to the worst school in
the entire solar system. The PE teacher, Coach
Mutton, never started a class without a box of
jelly doughnuts—in fact, he pretty much never
started a class.

I'LL TRADE YOU THIS JELLY DOUGHNUT FOR SOME OF THAT PEZ, SON.

The cafeteria was loaded with junk food.

HERE'S A NICE PEZ AND CHEX MIX SANDWICH, DEAR.

The teachers, for the most part, were bused in from the local senior citizens' home, and taught very little besides crafts, bingo, and shuffleboard.

TODAY, BOYS AND GIRLS, WE'RE GOING TO LEARN HOW TO MAKE THIS HANDY TWINE HOLDER.

IT'LL BE GOOD TO BE BACK.

I CAN'T WAIT.

13

There had been one teacher, Mr. Bomzie, otherwise known as the Horrible, Hideous History Teacher, who actually taught something, but he turned out to be a zombie, and Fred and Anthony had managed to get rid of him in their second book.

Mrs. Kissis, who was the only teacher in the entire school under eighty, replaced Mr. Bomzie. She never gave tests or homework, and she let everybody eat Pez and Chex Mix.

IT'S GOING TO BE A GREAT YEAR.

THE BEST.

THERE WAS ONLY ONE OTHER THING. . . .

But Fred and Anthony didn't let even the Heinie Goblin who had followed them out of the Netherworld from the last book ruin their positive state of mind.

They had received copies of their new book just in time for the first day of school, and the boys were eager to show them off to everybody.

19

with a spring in their step and a smile on their faces, carrying copies of their new book, Fred and Anthony waited in anticipation for the bus that would take them to school.

BUS STOP

WHEN WE WALK INTO THAT SCHOOL WITH COPIES OF THIS BOOK, PEOPLE ARE GOING TO FINALLY RESPECT US!

AWESOME.

Little did they know, on that sparkling September morning, what startling changes had occurred over the summer, which were about to set off a horrible chain of events for them.

DID YOU HEAR THAT?

IT'S ALWAYS SOMETHING.

To begin with, Coach Mutton was gone!

YES!

Colonel Chilblain was the new gym teacher. He was on a fanatical rampage to eliminate body fat and increase muscle mass in every single kid on the planet Earth—a teacher who loathed Pez and Chex Mix and worshipped broccoli rabe—a teacher who lived in constant fear of getting thirsty and had strapped to his back a hydration pack with a hands-free water bladder.

Was he even human?

WHAT'S THIS?

GET YOUR HANDS OFF MY BLADDER.

HE SAID "BLADDER."

Colonel Chilblain made sure there was no junk food in the cafeteria.

HERE'S A NICE ARUGULA-AND-OATMEAL SANDWICH, DEAR.

THE NEXT THING YOU KNOW, MRS. KISSIS WILL BE GONE, TOO.

As if that weren't bad enough, Mrs. Kissis was gone, too!

In her place was a new teacher—a teacher who demanded perfection—who deplored bingo, line dancing, watching soap operas, and wood shop.

HELLO, BOYS AND GIRLS. I'M YOUR NEW TEACHER.

MRS. QUIZZUS

Mrs. Quizzus was a teacher who was in love with tests and grades, as well as orthopedic footwear, and owned several pairs of Earth shoes.

Was *she* even human?

TAKE OUT YOUR PAPER AND PENS— I'M GIVING YOU A TEST.

BUT WE HAVEN'T LEARNED ANY- THING YET.

SO WHAT!

But Mrs. Quizzus and Colonel Chilblain were too distracted to fully appreciate the boys' status as characters in a chapter book series.

In fact, everyone was excited that day. After years of parents' selling their houses and moving to another district just to get their kids out of the school, for the first time in history, Sunny Babbling Brook Elementary had something it had never had before.

A NEW STUDENT

Billy Bob was his name. He was as cute as a button and polite as all get-out, with an angelic smile and a better-than-average ability to tap-dance.

Fred and Anthony took an immediate disliking to the new kid. So did the creepy janitor, who lived in the mop closet and was stark raving mad.

30

Meanwhile, Fred and Anthony could hardly get anybody to even look at their book.

YOU CALL THIS A BOOK? DON'T MAKE ME LAUGH!

FRED & ANTHONY ESCAPE from the NETHERWORLD

But that wasn't the worst of Fred and Anthony's troubles, because right away a series of mysterious accidents began to occur.

and had to perform the Heimlich maneuver on himself.

three cheerleaders were mysteriously over-come by toxic mold that formed on their pom-poms, the first graders got mysteriously stuck together by psychomagnetic slime that poured through the hallways, and one of the cafeteria ladies sprained her wrist when her body was mysteriously inhabited by a monster from outer space.

It could only be one thing that was causing the trouble at Sunny Babbling Brook Elementary: a disgruntled spirit from the Netherworld.

39

BOOMZILLE?!
COME ON, LET'S GO GET HIS AUTOGRAPH AND SELL IT ON e-BAY!

As it turned out, Billy Bob Bomzie *was* from the Netherworld—just like the stark raving mad janitor had warned—and Billy Bob had every reason to be disgruntled. For one thing, he was the son of Mr. Bomzie, the Horrible, Hideous History Teacher, who had gotten eaten by the Giant Slimy Snot Sandwich–Eating Fungus Blob. For another thing, Fred and Anthony were the two responsible for this—and if you had read the second book, you'd know that by now.

Clearly Billy Bob was the culprit, but he was blaming Fred and Anthony for the rash of mysterious accidents!

Angered by a purple pinky toe, putrid pom-poms, stuff pouring through the halls, and a sprained wrist, an angry mob formed.

Fred and Anthony ran for their lives up one hallway and down the next, through the psychomagnetic slime, which was sort of like that yellow watery stuff floating on the top of a cup of yogurt that you're supposed to mix in but that you always pour off because you're so grossed out.

Billy Bob and the angry mob chased Fred and Anthony—who, on the bright side, after three books of running for their lives, were finally starting to get into shape.

46

47

THE PHANTOM from the MOP CLOSET

In the nick of time, Fred and Anthony were offered shelter by the kindly yet misunderstood creepy janitor, who was really a phantom.

The Phantom explained that he had taken the job at Sunny Babbling Brook Elementary in order to get over a failed love affair in the Netherworld.

But he had urgent news for the boys! There wasn't a moment to lose, because Billy Bob Bomzie had abducted Mrs. Kissis and Coach Mutton, who were being held captive in the Netherworld!

THAT'S TERRIBLE—BUT I DO LOVE WHAT YOU'VE DONE WITH THIS MOP CLOSET.

YEAH—IT'S REAL HOMEY.

THANKS! BUT YOU MUST COME WITH ME—HURRY!

53

But before the Phantom could tell the boys anything else, he was sucked inside his own television—which seems highly unlikely but is exactly what happened!

Not

58

Without a single thought for their own well-being, Fred and Anthony rushed to the aid of the beloved teachers.

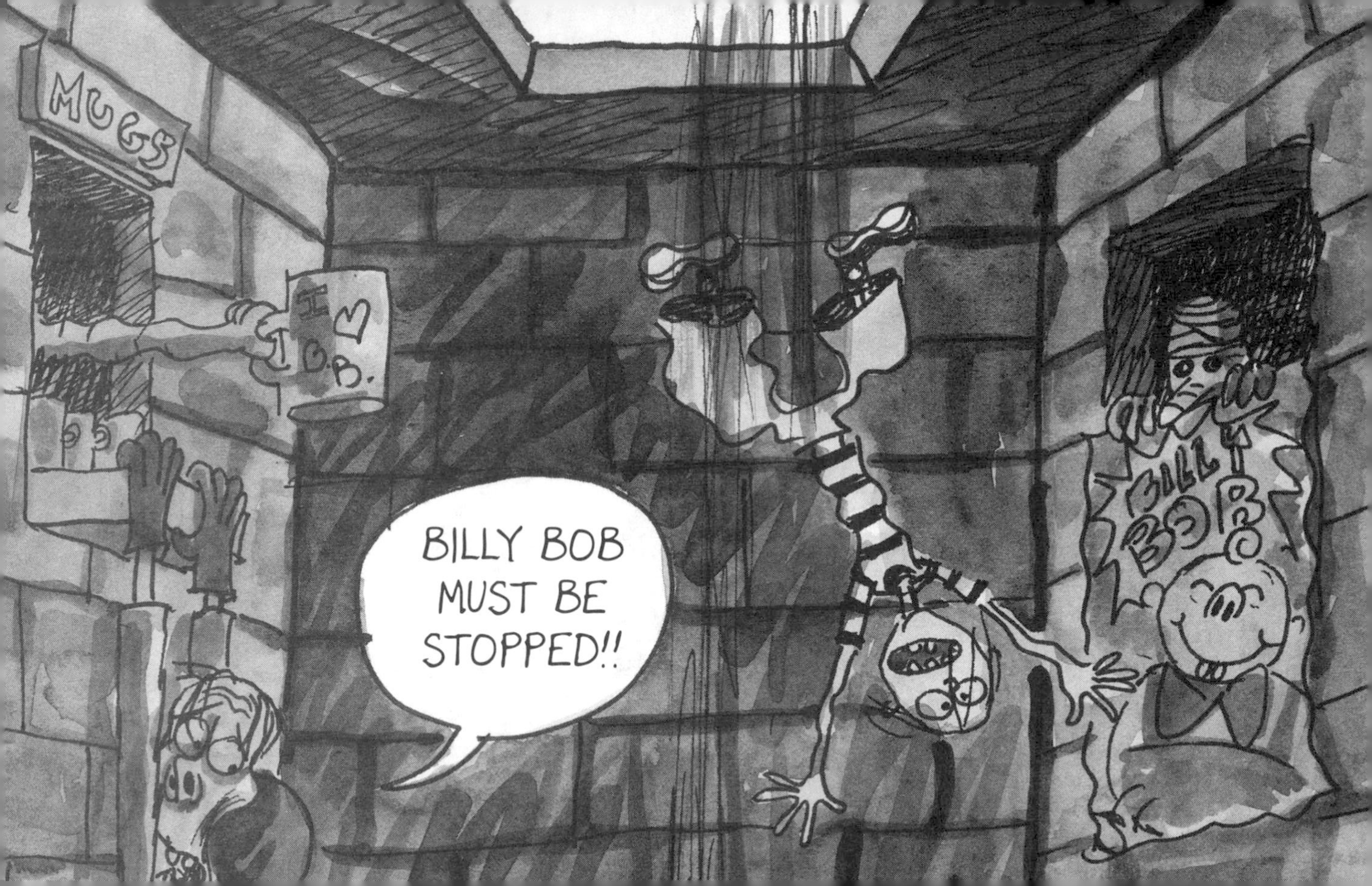
MUGS
I ♥ B.B.
BILLY BOB MUST BE STOPPED!!
BILLY BOB

65

Fred and Anthony were back in the Netherworld, and right away they were in the clutches of a most horrible, hideous character.

If only the boys had not been so lazy, they would never have been driven to increase their cash flow to pay other kids to do their work for them, and right now they would be safe and sound in Fred's crummy basement. Instead, Fred's and Anthony's lives, as well as two so-so teachers and a phantom, were in peril.

YOU FED BILLY BOB BOMZIE'S FATHER TO A FUNGUS BLOB, AND NOW YOU'RE GONNA PAY!
PAY?
NO!

YES!

Boys and girls, it is hoped that you have learned from Fred and Anthony's misdeeds in that you will never ever EVER feed one of your teachers to a fungus blob—no matter how horrible or hideous that teacher is!

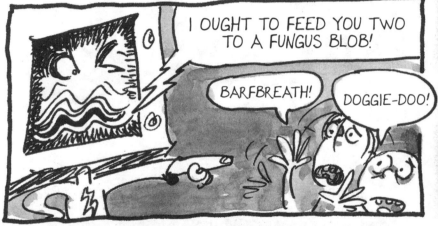

♪ DING-DONG ♪

Just when things looked their darkest for Fred and Anthony, the Giant Slimy Snot Sandwich–Eating Fungus Blob from the second book came knocking on the Dark Force's door. He was there to complain that he had forked over his life savings hoping to become popular and meet that special someone, but it had not happened.

Faced with a lifetime of bachelorhood and bad take-out Chinese food, the Fungus Blob took hold of Dark Force.

Thus the lives of Fred and Anthony were saved.

Suddenly Billy Bob Bomzie appeared. Upset that not only had his father been fed to a Fungus Blob but now his Dark Force had too, Billy Bob was ready to exact his revenge.

After three books of escaping the Netherworld and its various dangers, the boys had avoided being debrained and desanitized; they had survived being eaten by the creature from the Black Lagoon; and they had even managed not to be annoyed to death by Heinie Goblins. But their most unspeakable trial had yet to befall them!

In the cruelest form of mind-numbing horror, the boys were made to transform the Dark Force's office to cleverly simulate Fred's basement. Fred and Anthony would now be bringing Billy Bob packs of Pez, bowls of Chex Mix, and Purell hand-sanitizer on and on into infinity. And if you had read the second book, you'd know why Billy Bob was going through Purell like there was no tomorrow.

THEY'D ALSO KNOW WHY I HAVE A NICE LEMONY FRESH SCENT.

Fred and Anthony were doomed, all right. The only thing that could save them now was a miracle.

A SERIES of MIRACLES

9

And why not? Fred and Anthony had survived ghosts, monsters, blood, and guts for the last three books, not to mention fourth-grade square dancing. Perhaps hoping for a miracle wasn't out of the realm of possibility!

81

83

Poor Fred and Anthony—there would be no miracles for them. Instead they found themselves in a hot, stuffy room sitting around a table with fruit cups and chicken Murphy at a beastly awards banquet listening to Billy Bob's endless acceptance speech while he tap-danced.

Everyone in the Netherworld was as in love with Billy Bob as they had been at Sunny Babbling Brook Elementary. They were so in love with him, in fact, they could have eaten him up.

TAP   TAP

91

Yes, Billy Bob was gone, but Colonel Chilblain and Mrs. Quizzus, as well as everyone from the Netherworld who Fred and Anthony had ever ticked off over the course of the last three books, were still there at the banquet and took the opportunity to exact their revenge.

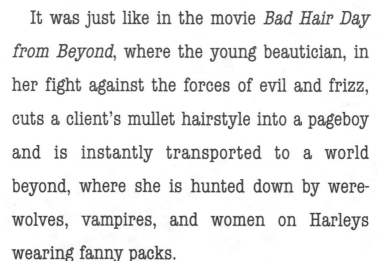

It was just like in the movie *Bad Hair Day from Beyond*, where the young beautician, in her fight against the forces of evil and frizz, cuts a client's mullet hairstyle into a pageboy and is instantly transported to a world beyond, where she is hunted down by werewolves, vampires, and women on Harleys wearing fanny packs.

Fred and Anthony ran for their lives down into the bowels of the banquet building, and if you'd read the first book, you would be used to the word "bowels" by now and wouldn't think it was at all funny.

I READ THE FIRST BOOK, AND I STILL THINK "BOWELS" IS FUNNY.

MOP CLOSET

PSSST! OVER HERE!

Luckily for Fred and Anthony, in what could be considered nothing other than a happy twist of fate, they were found by the Phantom from the Mop Closet, who had been looking all over for them since page 62.

MORE HAPPY TWISTS of FATE 11

The Phantom sprang into action. With Fred under one arm and Anthony under the other, he ran like crazy.

Fred and Anthony soon learned that their two dear teachers had been held captive since September at the Little Monster Middle School, where the Phantom used to work and still had a mop closet. Mrs. Kissis was being tortured by having to make lesson plans, give tests, and teach.

Coach Mutton was being forced to lay off the doughnuts, stay in the gym, and hold Phys. Ed. classes.

As they hurried to the school, the boys wondered—
were the teachers alive or dead?

But they didn't have to wait for long—because coming toward them were Mrs. Kissis and Coach Mutton, who were ashen and shaken but, thankfully, still alive.

As glad as everyone was to see one another, there was no time for talk. The boys and their teachers were in terrible danger, and as usual, the Phantom came to the rescue.

He loaded them into a nearby coffinmobile, which is a contraption that you might think was made up conveniently for this part of the story but was really a happy twist of fate.

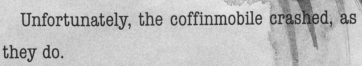

Unfortunately, the coffinmobile crashed, as they do.

. . . for a Jeep Grand Cherokee.

And the group took off down the road for the Little Monster Middle School and the Phantom's mop closet, where they could make their way to safety.

Yes, boys and girls, it had been a long forty-six pages, and everyone was more than ready to leave the Netherworld.

On the other hand, it was heartening for Fred and Anthony to see someone who was actually in worse shape than they were.

IF I EVER GET OUT OF HERE ALIVE, I WILL NEVER HAVE BLUE CHEESE DRESSING ON MY DOUGHNUTS EVER AGAIN.

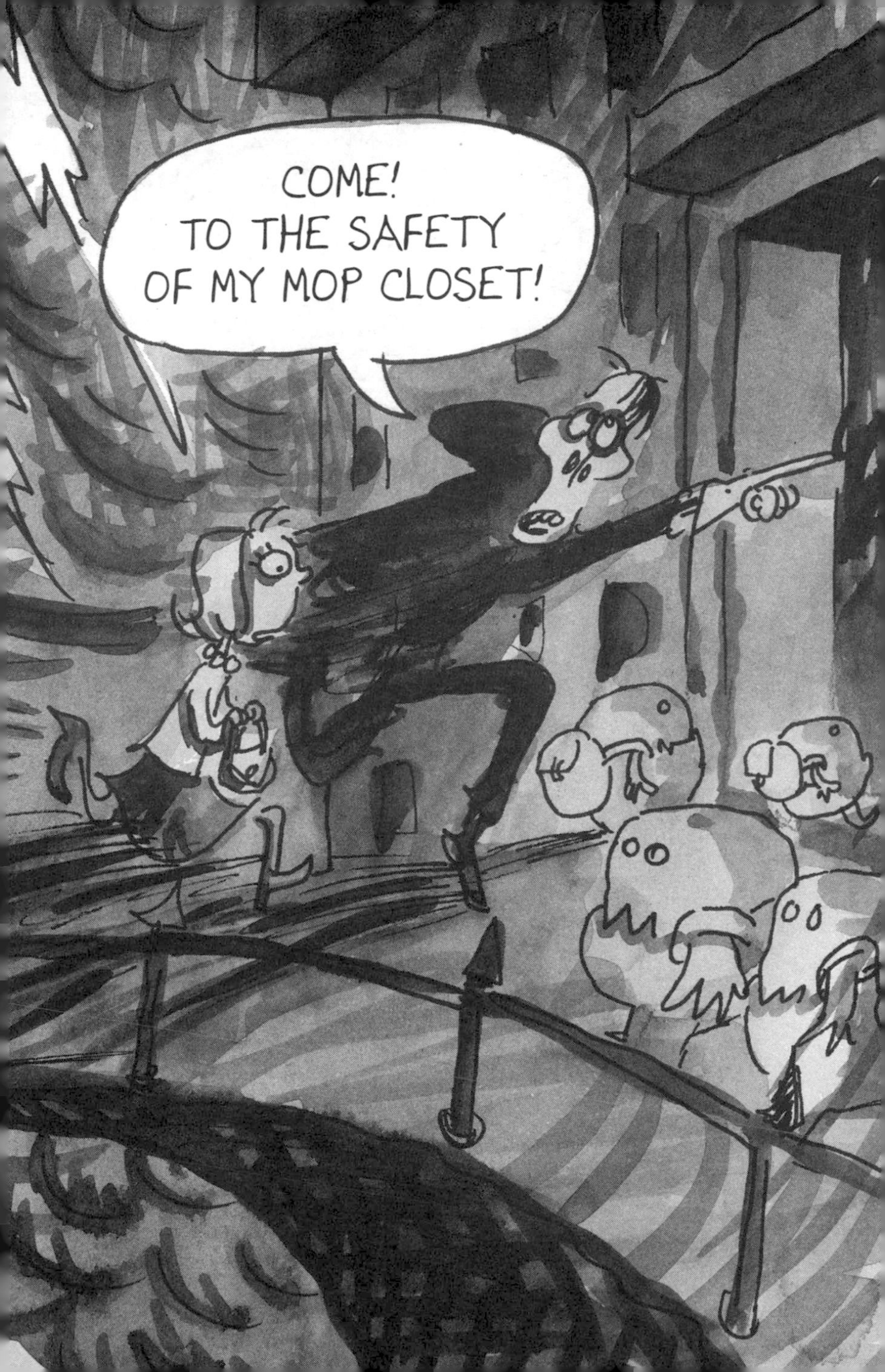
COME!
TO THE SAFETY
OF MY MOP CLOSET!

Once again, Fred and Anthony had narrowly escaped from the Netherworld and wound up inside their own TV, which may make absolutely no sense whatsoever, but the boys still had more happy twists of fate coming to them—winding up inside their own TV being one.

LET US OUT OF HERE!

As much as they hated to admit it, Fred and Anthony didn't think they could survive one more book of it.

Four books of falling into the Netherworld had finally taken its toll on the boys.

I THINK I'M COMING DOWN WITH SOMETHING.

GUIDE to the NETHERWORLD SURGEON GENERAL'S WARNING!

More than three trips to the Netherworld may be hazardous to your health and could result in a violent death.

THIS MADNESS MUST STOP!

Because of their desire to stay alive, the boys'
hopes and dreams of making a fortune with
their children's book series had vanished.

Always remember, though, kids, steel is tempered by fire, and Fred and Anthony had come through their trials and tribulations better boys. They took this latest disappointment with maturity and grace, like the strong young men they now were.

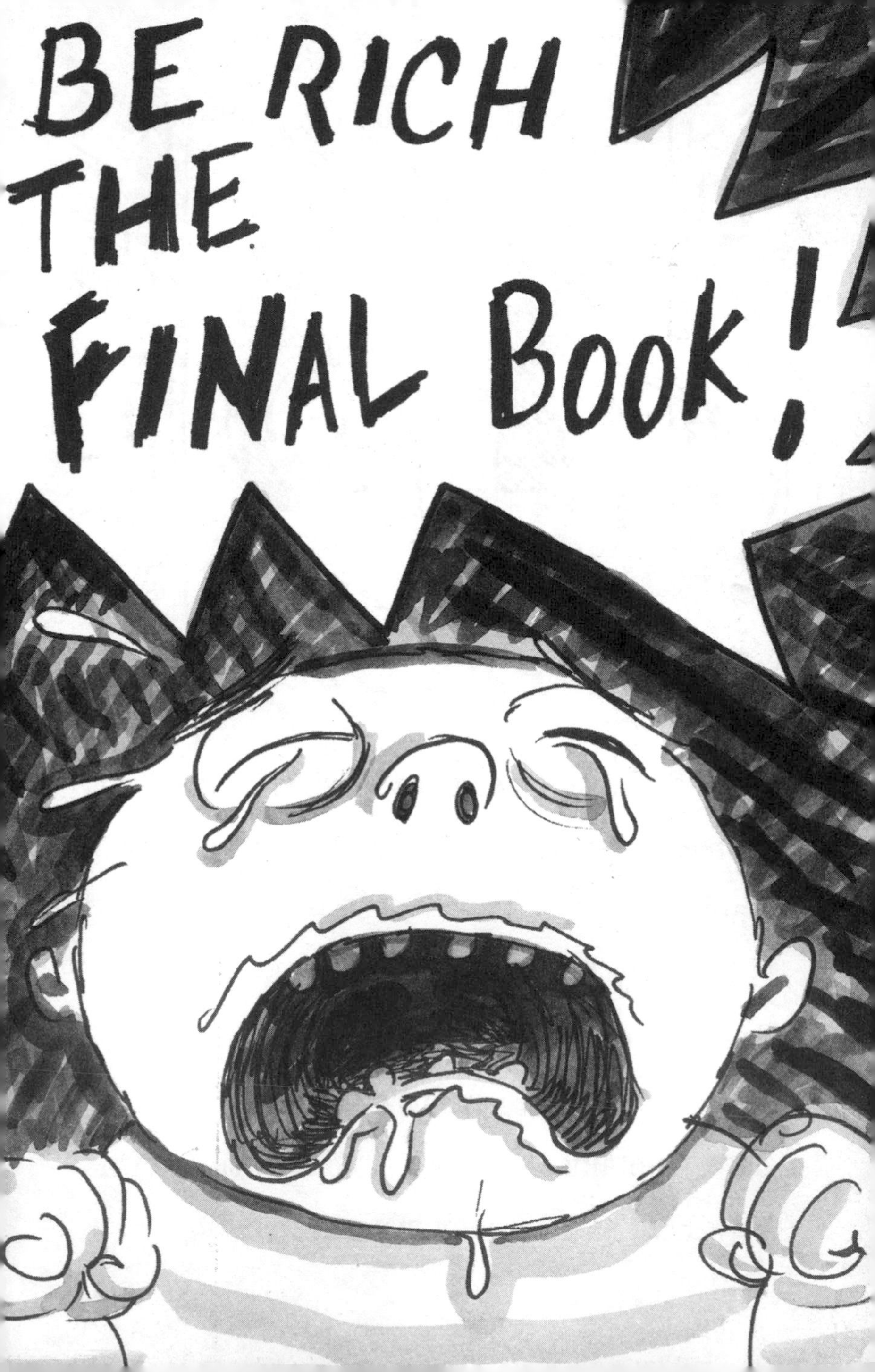
BE RICH
THE
FINAL Book!

And so this story ends as it began, with Fred and Anthony eating Pez and Chex Mix and watching TV.

No, they weren't as rich as the Queen of England and didn't live in mansions, or have butlers bringing them bowls of Chex Mix or have fountains spewing Pez, but in their own way, Fred and Anthony were happy.

Mrs. Kissis and Coach Mutton had their old jobs restored at Sunny Babbling Brook Elementary, and soon thereafter, startling changes began to occur!

The two teachers had come to see things in a whole new light.

Having survived the Netherworld, they decided that with every fiber of their beings, they would make good and devote the rest of their lives to improving the minds and bodies of all the little children entrusted to their care.

Crafts, bingo, line dancing, watching soap operas, and wood shop were replaced with reading, writing, arithmetic, and consuming large quantities of water, broccoli rabe, and arugula.

Needless to say, you couldn't find a pack of
Pez or a bowl of Chex Mix anywhere inside the
school to save your life.

Sure, Coach Mutton and Mrs. Kissis had been transformed into creatures from the Netherworld as a result of their trip, but for the first time in history, every student at Sunny Babbling Brook Elementary would be fully hydrated, and have low body fat and high IQ's.

In short, Sunny Babbling Brook Elementary was well on its way to becoming the best school on the planet Earth . . . if not the entire solar system!

ALLIN' ON MY HEAD, AND JUS

Now, *that's* scary.